C.J. WALKER BUILDS A BUSINESS

REBEL GIRLS

Our books are available at special quantity discounts for bulk purchase for sale promotions, premiums, fundraising, and educational needs. For details, write to sales@rebelgirls.co

Text: Denene Millner

Cover and Illustrations: Salini Perera

Cover Lettering: Monique Aimee

FSC
www.fsc.org
MIX
Paper from
responsible sources
FSC® C013123

This is a work of historical fiction. We have tried to be as accurate as possible, but names, characters, businesses, places, events, locales, and incidents may have been changed to suit the needs of the story.

www.rebelgirls.co

ISBN 978-1-7331761-9-4

MORE BOOKS
FROM REBEL GIRLS . . .

Good Night Stories for Rebel Girls

•

Good Night Stories for Rebel Girls 2

•

I Am a Rebel Girl:
A Journal to Start Revolutions

•

Ada Lovelace Cracks the Code

To the Rebel Girls of the world...

Forge your own path,
and make it your truth.

Madam C. J. Walker (Sarah Breedlove Walker)

December 23, 1867 - May 25, 1919

United States of America

CHAPTER ONE

Mama parted Sarah's hair into three sections: one in the front, two in the back. Sarah wiggled as Mama started at the root and worked her way to the ends. She loved feeling her mama's fingers in her hair.

"Sit *still*, wiggle worm," Mama said. Sarah's older sister, Louvenia, sat off to the side, scratching her freshly-done braids. She made faces at Sarah until Mama gave Lou a sharp look. "Cut it out, Lou. Sweep the porch if you ain't got nothing better to do."

Sarah Breedlove, the littlest of five siblings, was her family's hope for the future. Born in 1867, she was the first member of her family who hadn't been born into slavery. Now she would be the first to go to school.

Even though Sarah was only five years old, last harvest season she had bent down right next to Mama, Papa, Lou, and her three older brothers, Alexander, Owen, and James. The whole family had pulled fluffy cotton planted in neat rows that stretched beyond the horizon. Sarah remembered sweating in the hot sun. Sometimes the prickly parts of the plants would poke right through her fingers. But Sarah kept right on working, filling her bag no matter how heavy it got. She knew her family could not survive without it.

After her hair was close to perfect, Mama put Sarah to bed and hummed a lullaby.

"You, chile, are going to school tomorrow. No more cotton picking for my baby. You'll be bigger than all these fields. Bigger than the Mississippi River."

The thought made Sarah smile as she drifted off to sleep.

The Breedloves couldn't always pay for what they needed, like food, shoes, or home repairs.

During the winter, cold air crept through gaps in the rough wooden walls where the slats did not quite meet. But that year's cotton harvest had been bountiful. The whole family got new clothes and shoes, and Pa finally bought oil to fix the squeaky cabin door. Best of all, Mama and Papa could finally get married!

"It costs a hundred dollars to tie the knot," Mama said, grinning as she shook the rattling jam jar. "Guess how many dollars I got here?"

"A hundred!" Sarah and Louvenia chorused, dancing their way around Mama's feet.

They held the ceremony right there in the backyard under the trees. Mama's eyes sparkled as she stood in her best dress, holding Papa's hands.

The pastor sweated, fanning himself as he read from his big, black book.

Sarah squeezed Louvenia's hand on one side and her brother Alexander's on the other. "Pastor looks like he swallowed a bug," she whispered.

"Shhh!" hissed Louvenia.

Alexander's body shook as he snorted to keep from laughing.

After the ceremony, out came rickety tables and chairs scattered across the grass. The whole neighborhood filled the yard, bringing piles of food that made Sarah's mouth water. An old man strummed on a banjo sitting in the cool shade. Children shrieked with delight, playing hand-clapping games in the field nearby.

Then came Mama's cake: sweet and thick with crinkles at the top. Mama sliced a piece special for Sarah. As she let the sugar dissolve on her tongue, Sarah felt that life, like Mama's cake, was the sweetest it could be.

~

On the first day of school, Mama wrapped up a biscuit in a piece of cloth and tucked it into Sarah's pocket. Then Papa walked her down the road to the schoolhouse.

Sarah's heart beat faster when she let go of Papa's

hand and stepped into a dimly lit room with wide open windows. She marched right up to her teacher and introduced herself: "Hello, ma'am. I'm Sarah Breedlove."

"Why hello, Sarah! It's lovely to meet you. I'm Mrs. Peacott." The teacher led Sarah to an empty table.

Sarah perched on a wooden bench and picked up her very own piece of chalk.

Sarah loved school. She loved how the chalk slid across the board. She loved learning how to form letters and numbers in wobbly lines at first and then in careful swirls.

But Sarah's education ended as quickly as it had begun.

After only three months, the state of Louisiana decided not to spend money on school for black children like Sarah. Hundreds of children went back to work in the fields, never to become politicians, lawyers, or business owners. But Sarah had learned a valuable lesson in the classroom: to dream of possibility.

CHAPTER TWO

Louvenia took all that Sarah owned and put it in the middle of a scratchy wool blanket on their parents' bed: a metal cup, a small plate, Sarah's Sunday dress, Papa's work scarf, and Mama's spoon. These few belongings were all that was left now that Sarah's parents had passed away.

As Louvenia was about to tie the blanket into a sack to make it easier to carry, Sarah grabbed Papa's work scarf and held it to her nose. It smelled like his sweat after a long day's work, thick and earthy. The scent brought fresh tears to Sarah's eyes.

At eight years old, Sarah became an orphan and had to leave the only home she'd ever known to live with her older sister Louvenia, her brother-in-law Jesse, and her baby nephew Willie.

Sarah had barely set down her sack in her new home when Jesse stood over her. She felt a shiver travel down her spine.

"You can stay here, but you're going to earn your keep," Jesse told her. "You will clean the house, cook breakfast, pick cotton, and watch your nephew. You can find washing work in town, too."

Doing laundry was the hardest job of all. Every morning, Sarah carried clothes to the river and scrubbed them clean against a wooden washboard. Then she struggled up the slope with the wet clothes weighing on her small body. She reached up high to pin them on the clothesline to dry.

The next day, she had to do it all over again.

On Sundays, Sarah felt a little spark of joy when she got to see her brothers at church. Even then, they only managed a quick hug after service. Jesse snapped at her to hurry up so that she could get her chores done.

James bristled when he heard the impatience in Jesse's voice. "Stay strong, little sister," he whispered.

The pennies Sarah earned didn't make up for the fact that work was getting scarce in their small town. The family hoped to make a better living in nearby Vicksburg, Mississippi. They moved but life wasn't much different, Sarah realized.

~

"Sarah!" Alexander tugged Sarah into a warm hug.

All of Sarah's brothers had moved to Vicksburg, too. Alexander had a good job at a grocery store, stocking shelves, mopping floors, and helping customers with heavy bags. He worked hard but he still had some time for his baby sister.

"You're late," Alexander chuckled, turning the grocery store sign from open to closed.

Sarah grinned and grabbed his hand. "Come on. Let's go!"

Brother and sister stepped out into the sunlight. Sarah peered in all the shop windows. She wondered what it would be like to sit on a sofa with cushions soft as clouds. She wanted to pluck a feather from one of the hats on display and feel it glide across her fingers. What if she could wear shoes so shiny she could see her face in them?

A steamboat horn thundered, making Sarah's body rumble. She watched the boat chug up the river and wondered where it was headed. She hoped that it was going somewhere magical, to a place where no one went to bed hungry and little girls could go to school instead of working so hard.

"Sarah," Alexander said, setting a heavy hand on her shoulder. "I'm leaving Vicksburg soon."

"Leaving? But you just got here!"

"Don't look at me like that." Alexander's face got so serious that the center of his forehead wrinkled. "It's not safe for me here anymore. We're going to St. Louis where there's more black people and hopefully less lynching."

Sarah didn't say a word. She knew what happened to black people sometimes. She knew white men got angry and rode their horses around: burning houses and churches, yelling, even killing black people. Mama and Papa had called it "lynching." She'd heard them whispering, but they'd stopped whenever Sarah got near. They hadn't wanted her to know about those things.

"C'mon, lil sis." Alexander's voice got soft and low as he tugged her along the riverbank. "Let's get something from the sweet shop. What would you like?"

"Peppermint?" Sarah asked in a small voice.

"Peppermint it is."

A few weeks later, Alexander, James, and Owen headed to St. Louis, Missouri, to find work in a barbershop. Her brothers all kissed Sarah goodbye and promised to write.

But her heart ached, just like when Mama and Papa died.

CHAPTER THREE

Sarah dreamed she was sitting on the porch in Papa's lap, with Mama close by. The three of them gazed at the stars . . .

"Get up!" Jesse growled, startling Sarah out of her sleep. Jesse snatched the small wool cover off Sarah's body and tossed it to the floor. "You gonna sleep the day away? Get out there, gather the eggs, and fix me some breakfast. I won't stand any laziness in my house! Lazy girls don't deserve to eat."

The day before, Sarah had awoken before the sun rose to churn butter, prepare breakfast, and haul laundry down to the river, and she'd worked hard until long after it had set. But that didn't matter. Every day was the same.

Sarah's brothers still hadn't sent for her, so she needed to find a way out of her misery on her own. But Sarah was only fourteen and couldn't afford to live alone yet. The quickest way was to share the burden of earning a living with someone else. She thought she knew of someone.

She put her plan into action at the next church fish fry.

"Miss Olive, let me take my turn at serving," Sarah said, stepping in to take the spoon. For a few months, she'd had her eye on a nice young man at her church named Moses. And now here he was, waiting in the serving line.

"Hi, Miss Sarah," Moses said with a big ole smile on his face.

Moses admired how kind and eager Sarah was. She was always the first to raise her hand to answer questions at Bible study, and the first to volunteer at bake sales. He loved her wide brown eyes and how her smooth skin glowed in the sunlight.

"Hi yourself, Moses. I fixed this special for you," Sarah said sweetly. She handed him a plate heaped high with fish, field peas, cornbread, and pickled watermelon.

It didn't take long for Sarah to convince Moses she'd be the perfect partner.

Within weeks, Sarah and Moses snuck off to get married. The young couple exchanged vows, took each other's hands, then jumped over a brightly-decorated broom handle together. This was called "jumping the broom" just like Sarah's parents had when it was illegal for slaves to get married.

~

Sarah liked her new life. Although she missed her sister, she didn't miss Jesse's yelling. Moses had two good crop seasons in a row, allowing Sarah to breathe a little easier. They had extra money to buy what they needed and even some of what they wanted.

Each night, Moses came home, set his boots by the door, and greeted his wife. One night, he brought home two peppermints sticks: Sarah's favorite!

"What's the special occasion?" Sarah laughed as she held the sticky candy.

"To remind you how sweet life is when we're together," Moses said.

Three years later, Sarah and Moses had a baby girl named Lelia. Sarah adored her daughter. She wanted to build a world around Lelia full of joy and kindness.

"Good morning, sunshine!" she sang every morning, bouncing Lelia on her knee.

Sarah especially loved her baby's hair because it was nothing like her own. Sarah's hair was dry, crunchy, and itchy. She wished she had the tools she needed to style it. Though even if she did, she didn't know any hairstyles to try. It was thin and kept falling out, so she wrapped it up in a big piece of fabric.

Sarah worried that Leila's hair would end up like hers, so she tried to protect it. Once a week, she sat Lelia on her lap and combed out the tangles in her baby's hair. Then she styled it into little puffs tied with brightly-colored ribbons.

Sarah remembered how good it felt to have her Mama play with her hair. It felt like love, and she wanted Lelia to feel that, too.

"I'm going to make your dreams come true, little baby," she whispered into Lelia's ear.

For a while, it seemed those dreams were possible. Then Sarah's happiness came to an end. One night, her beloved Moses went out to a meeting and did not return.

Sarah rocked Lelia to sleep and sat anxiously by the door, waiting to hear her husband's footsteps on the porch. The hours ticked by and still, no Moses.

The next morning, Sarah received the terrible news. Moses had been killed, and someone whispered that word again: "Lynching."

Just like that, Sarah was a widow at age twenty with a toddler to raise by herself.

~

After Moses was buried, Sarah knew she had to leave Vicksburg. She bought two tickets on a boat headed north up the Mississippi River.

Sarah sat on the floor in the belly of the boat

among the pigs, sheep, and goats. It was the only space onboard she could afford. Everything she owned was wrapped in a blanket once more. She held Leila tight in her arms, cupping her little daughter's head against her chest, trying to drown out the throb of the engine.

After a while, they both fell asleep to the rocking of the boat.

CHAPTER FOUR

S t. Louis, Missouri, was unlike any place Sarah had ever seen! She nearly hurt her neck standing on the sidewalk to gaze up at the tall buildings. She heard words in languages she'd never known existed. Her attention jumped from store to store and person to person as she tried to take it all in. She wondered what it would be like to have dinner at a restaurant instead of having to cook every meal. She gaped at the tiny train called a "streetcar" that shuttled people to and from their destinations like a colorful steel horse.

St. Louis felt big, electric!

The first place Sarah went was her brothers' barbershop. "I'm so proud of you!" she cried and looked around, beaming. Every mirror in the place smiled back.

Alexander plucked Lelia out of Sarah's arms and held her up in the air, laughing. "Well aren't you pretty, lil peanut!"

Lelia giggled back.

"We're glad you're here, Sarah, but it's tough to make a city living. What will you do for work?" James asked.

"I'll be a barber just like you," Sarah teased.

"You can if you put your mind to it," Owen piped up.

Sarah was grateful for her brothers' encouragement and hopeful for her future. But without an education, she could only work the same jobs she had before. With a sigh, Sarah went back to washing laundry and cleaning houses.

Sarah made just a dollar a day so she lived in the only place she could afford: the Badlands. The Badlands was the most polluted, dangerous part of St. Louis. But Sarah found joy, despite it all. She joined a church and made new friends. Her friends told her about an affordable school for Lelia.

Sarah worked harder than she had in her entire life to make sure her daughter received the education she never had. Sixteen years flew by. Lelia thrived at school and went on to earn top grades. Sitting in the audience at Lelia's high school graduation, Sarah thought this had to be the proudest she'd ever felt.

Then Lelia got accepted at Knoxville College in Tennessee!

Like her Mama had scraped coins together in jam jars to pay for a wedding, Sarah made sure Lelia had enough for her tuition. She was determined her daughter would never have to work as a washerwoman, and encouraged her to get a beauty degree.

While shopping for Lelia's college supplies, Sarah spotted a bottle that made her stomach turn. It had a picture on the front showing a black woman with kinky hair next to what looked like a white woman with straight hair. "You too can be beautiful!" the label read.

"They're calling us ugly," Sarah grumbled, stomping down the aisle to show Lelia the bottle. "Just look at this shampoo!"

Lelia's nose wrinkled in disgust. "I don't want that, Mama."

"That's the only shampoo there is, baby," her mother replied.

Sarah reluctantly dropped the bottle in her basket.

~

With Lelia away at college, Sarah had more time to herself. She enrolled in night school. There, she learned reading, math, geography, and bookkeeping. On the weekends, she volunteered at an organization dedicated to helping the poor.

At one meeting, Sarah passed around a newspaper with a headline that read: "Local Man Struggles to Care for Family."

"We should host a bake sale for this man," Sarah said. She remembered what it felt like to go hungry.

Sometimes she hadn't even had so much as a handful of grits for breakfast.

The following Sunday, everyone brought a little something to sell. Jenny made crackling bread. Thelma baked a pie with fresh blackberries. Sarah recreated her mother's wedding cake. The desserts sold faster than they could put slices on the plates!

Sarah's fundraiser was such a success that the local paper wanted to run a story on it.

One of the newspaper journalists, Charles Walker, invited Sarah into a small office full of piles of paper covered in scribblings. The typewriter keys on the desk looked so well worn, Sarah wondered how many words he typed in a day.

"It's a pleasure to finally meet you, Ms. Breedlove," Charles said. "I've heard so many good things about your work."

"Why thank you, Mr. Walker," said Sarah. "The pleasure is all mine."

Charles's handshake was firm and sure, and Sarah liked him right away. He was smart and ambitious, and funny, too! They went on a few dates. Charles always dressed formally whether it was the weekend or a workday, and Sarah teased him about his love of matching bow ties and socks. Soon after, they became a couple.

Sarah now had a new boyfriend, a daughter in college, and a happy, busy life. She started getting invitations to events sponsored by well-to-do black people. But Sarah was not completely comfortable at these gatherings. She felt she stood out, and not in a good way.

The women at the parties had fancier clothes, lighter skin, and long, shiny hair. Sarah had dark brown skin and while she was not ashamed of her skin, her hair was another story. Sarah's hair was kinky and short, with flaky bald spots. No matter how hard she tried, she could *not* get her hair to grow.

Sarah decided to make her hair so beautiful that she never had to cover it or feel ashamed of it again.

CHAPTER FIVE

S arah dropped another clothespin into the metal bucket and creased the fold of a crisp white pillowcase. There was a knock at the door.

A smartly dressed woman stood on Sarah's porch with a huge suitcase beside her. Smiling brown eyes peered out from behind a pair of round glasses. Sarah noticed that the woman's hair was pinned behind her head, but it looked shiny and healthy. "Hello. I'm Annie Turnbo. May I have a few minutes of your time?"

Sarah looked at Annie skeptically. But curiosity got the best of her so she let the woman inside. Annie had barely gotten through the door when she held up a small bottle and began talking a mile a minute.

"So you say it grows hair?" Sarah asked doubtfully,

turning the bottle over in her hands. She examined the label, reading the list of ingredients.

Many companies claimed to make products that grew black women's hair, but none of them really worked. And Sarah had had enough of being told she would only be beautiful if she looked like a white woman.

"It's not a straightener, is it?" she asked. "I like my hair kinky."

"Oh, I love kinky hair, too," Annie said. "This product won't *straighten* your hair. It will heal your scalp so that your hair grows."

"How does it do that?" Sarah asked.

"Why don't you come to my workshop?" Annie suggested. "I'll give you tips on how to make your hair healthier. In the meantime, let me wash your hair with my special shampoo. You'll love it!"

Sarah sat in a chair at her kitchen table while Annie filled a large bowl with water. Annie leaned Sarah's head back and gently rinsed her hair, added shampoo, then worked it into a lather. It was tingly at first, but Sarah loved how it calmed her itchy scalp. When Annie finished washing, drying, and combing Sarah's hair, it felt soft and fluffy instead of wiry and tangled.

"I'll definitely come to your class," Sarah said, handing Annie fifty cents for the rest of the shampoo.

~

Later that week, Sarah sat right in the front row so she wouldn't miss a thing.

"Clean scalps mean clean bodies. If you look good, people will think you're more accomplished. If you look accomplished, you'll get more business opportunities. More business opportunities lead to more money. And I don't have to tell you what you can do with more money!" Annie boasted, making everyone laugh. "The Wonderful Hair Grower will not only grow your hair, it will make you rich, ladies!"

The whole room hummed with excitement.

At the end of Annie's workshop, Sarah was ready to sign her name to become a Turnbo sales agent. As one of Annie's agents, she would earn double what she made now. She could quit washing clothes and still pay all her bills. There would even be a little extra cash left over to send to Lelia.

Sarah was convinced that selling Annie Turnbo's products would change her life. Plus, she wanted all the black women of St. Louis to look and feel good. Nothing, she decided, could be better than that.

CHAPTER SIX

In the two years since she'd started using Annie's products and practicing Turnbo beauty techniques, Sarah's scalp had gotten healthier. The flakes of dandruff practically disappeared, and so did the embarrassing bald spots. And wonder of wonders, Sarah's hair kept growing. First into a short, fluffy afro, and then into a longer, poofy one until it hung down to her shoulders. In fact, Sarah's hair was so glorious that she became a walking advertisement for Annie's products.

"Before I started using the Wonderful Hair Grower, my hair was only two inches long. Just look at me now!" Sarah told her clients. "You're going to want this for yourselves. I'll even let you try it for free. That's how much I believe in Annie Turnbo's Wonderful Hair Grower!"

Sarah became a top saleswoman in St. Louis and was richer than she'd ever been in her life.

As time went on, Sarah began to wonder if she could go into business for herself. She had already thought of ways to make a product even better than Annie's. But she knew Annie was not kind to those who tried to go into the hair business in St. Louis. Lately, Annie had been posting hurtful ads about new products and had tried to run other haircare sellers out of town. Secretly, Sarah stopped working as a Turnbo agent and started making plans to move to a city out of Annie's reach.

Sarah set her sights on Denver, Colorado, where her brother Owen now lived with his wife and their four daughters. She had received letter after letter about how the dry air caused her nieces' hair to become brittle, and about the lack of black hair care products in Denver. Sarah was convinced that Colorado was the place to make her start.

When she told Charles her decision, he was disappointed. But he understood and admired Sarah's passion to put her business first. They put their relationship on hold, and he promised to join her in Denver as soon as he could.

~

In Denver, Sarah worked as a cook in a boarding house. But her real work began when she got home each night.

First, she wrote down a list of ingredients she was sure would work well in her hair: coconut oil, petrolatum oil, and beeswax. She loved the smell of violet, so she added that to her list. Then she went to the store. Some of the items were on the shelves. Others she had to order.

As soon as she had all her ingredients, Sarah set to work in her kitchen. She reached for the biggest bowl she could find and a handful of long-handled spoons. Then she started mixing and stirring and stirring and mixing, looking like a mad scientist with a large curly afro.

Every now and then, she rubbed the paste she was making between her fingers and sniffed it, or slathered the cream onto a lock of her hair to see how it felt.

"Coconut oil and beeswax for softness. Geranium and violet for smell," she murmured to herself, changing the measurements from one tablespoon to two. Sarah kept adding ingredients then took them away. She scribbled notes, then crossed them out.

Sarah continued this process for months, until she had the perfect creaminess and smell. She parted her hair with a wide-toothed comb and massaged the final recipe into her scalp.

"Perfect!" she exclaimed to the empty kitchen. Though her apron was splattered with oil and paste, her scalp felt refreshed and her hair baby soft.

She'd done it!

Sarah couldn't wait to share her new recipe with the world. She placed an ad in the local black

newspaper and used herself as the before and after picture. She was confident that if she could show how well her product worked, she would have more clients than she knew what to do with.

Sure enough, customers from all over Colorado clamored to try her newest hair mixture. They all wanted to have their hair done by the marvelous Sarah Breedlove!

~

Eventually, Charles decided to join Sarah in the West. She put on her best dress, dabbed a little violet on her wrists, and headed over to the train station to meet him. The second he saw Sarah, Charles ran toward her with a big grin on his face.

"You're a sight for sore eyes," Sarah teased, tugging at his bow tie.

On the walk home, Sarah was nearly bursting with excitement as she told Charles everything she hadn't been able to express in her letters. She described difficult customers she'd met selling her hair products door to door. "One slammed the door right in my face. And now she's my best client!"

"Moving to Denver was a stroke of genius," Charles said, slowing down on the sidewalk. "You're a brilliant woman, Sarah Breedlove. Will you marry me?"

Sarah was overjoyed and nearly shouted the word "Yes!"

CHAPTER SEVEN

Sarah set up a shop and salon in her home so she could take clients and advertise her products. Business was good, but "Sarah's Wonderful Hair Grower" wasn't selling as well as Annie's well-known brand.

"Maybe it's because of the name," Sarah said to Charles one evening. She hunched over the kitchen table, pouring her sweet-smelling mixture into small round tins. "It should be more memorable."

"Well, I don't know about the name, but the ads with your picture got you a lot of customers," Charles said. "You should do that again."

"Oh yes, I planned on that," Sarah replied. She held up one of the tins to the light for closer inspection. "I think I'll put my picture on the tins, too."

"The ads are so elegant," Charles continued. "The name should match."

Sarah glanced over at him. Charles was sitting at the table in his suit complete with matching bow tie and socks. He always looked so elegant.

"I know!" Sarah said, snapping her fingers. "How about Madam C. J. Walker? Madam sounds important and high-quality, just like my product. And C. J. Walker sounds elegant."

"It sure does," Charles agreed.

"Then we've got a name!" Sarah said joyfully. "Madam C. J. Walker's Wonderful Hair Grower!"

After a few months of careful preparation, Sarah was ready. Under her new name, Madam C. J. Walker, she appeared in churches, community centers, and any place where black women gathered. Sarah began each session by telling the story of a dream that had started it all.

"A big black man appeared to me in a vision. He

began mixing and pouring. He didn't speak, but he showed me all the ingredients I needed. Some came from Africa, some from far away cities, and some from a plain old general store down the street! When I woke up, I wrote everything down as fast as I could." Sarah leaned toward her audience and lowered her voice as if letting them in on a secret. "And I thought, a gift like this should be shared. That's why I came here today, to share the magical formula with you all."

Sarah showed the women how to care for their hair, like Annie Turnbo had done for her. But this time, the product was Madam C. J. Walker's Wonderful Hair Grower. Sarah's audience just couldn't get enough of it! In fact, there were so many orders that Sarah could barely fill them. She needed an extra set of hands.

~

In 1906, fresh out of beauty college, Lelia came to her mother's rescue. At twenty-one, Lelia had grown into a charming and outspoken young woman, just like Sarah. Gone were the baby-fine curls and chubby cheeks, replaced by long, shiny locks and defined cheekbones. With a beauty degree in one hand and a list of brand-new hair techniques in the other, Lelia was ready to begin her career as a stylist.

Lelia had learned a new way of straightening hair using hot iron combs. The combs didn't make hair so brittle that it broke off, the way hair did when chemicals were used to straighten it. Best of all, women could simply wash their hair to go back to their kinky styles.

Lelia would spend an hour combing out each customer's afro, washing and drying it, then massaging the scalp with a mixture to protect it from burning under heat. Next, the iron comb went in the fire to get piping hot. Then Lelia carefully ran the steaming comb through the customer's hair.

"Hold your ear so I can get the edges," she'd instruct the woman sitting in the salon chair.

In no time, the customer's hair was straight and shiny and fell in gentle waves to her shoulders. Women would sometimes shriek with happiness and tip Lelia extra for the wonderful service.

Every person who left Lelia's chair felt beautiful. Those satisfied customers spread the word about Madam C. J. Walker's salon to anyone who would listen.

~

Soon, word of Sarah's success got back to her mentor and former boss, Annie Turnbo. Annie believed Sarah had stolen her recipe, slapped on a new label, and was taking credit for Turnbo products. Desperate to stop Sarah from stealing her customers, Annie took her fight to the newspapers.

"Beware of copycats," Annie warned. "Madam C. J. Walker would have been bald-headed if it weren't for my help!"

Sarah snorted in disgust. "Annie Turnbo is a liar if I ever heard one. She helped me get my start, but that's all she did. The rest I did on my own!"

Sarah responded by posting her own ad. Madam C. J. Walker declared that her product was the best of the best. Her hair grower was made with completely different ingredients than Annie's, and her results were faster. People all over the country believed in Madam C. J. Walker. Her sales numbers were strong, and business was booming.

A week later, Annie announced that one of *her* hair stylists would be setting up shop in Sarah's city.

Lelia nearly spit out her morning coffee when she heard the news. "Mama, what are we going to do? I'm good, but another shop could really hurt our business."

"I'm not worried, and you shouldn't be either." Sarah tossed the newspaper into the trash. "I have a plan."

CHAPTER EIGHT

A few weeks later, Sarah closed down her shop in Denver and hit the road.

Charles and Lelia went with her to continue packaging products and mailing them out to customers.

Who needs Denver? Sarah thought. *There are customers all over the country waiting for me!*

Even before her argument with Annie, Denver had begun to feel too small to Sarah. There weren't as many black people in Colorado as there were in the southern and eastern parts of the country.

Everywhere Sarah went, she taught women how to use the Walker Method and encouraged them to open up their own shops, selling Madam C. J.

Walker products. Her mission was to get as many women as she could to put down their washboards and pick up the ticket to prosperity.

After traveling through the South, the family of three headed up the East Coast to Pittsburgh. It was the perfect place to set up shop. Lelia took salon appointments and whipped up batches of hair creams in the evening. Charles packaged and mailed out orders as fast as they came in. Every day, Sarah worked toward building an army of saleswomen.

Each time she stood before a group of potential Walker Agents, Sarah chose her outfit carefully, so she looked like a boss.

Maids, cooks, and washerwomen leaned in like flowers toward the sun as Madam C. J. Walker spoke in her big, powerful voice. Sarah's puffy sleeves shook as she used her hands to punctuate each word. Unlike many of her students, she wore her hair uncovered and loose, which made everyone confident that her mixture worked.

"Growing hair is like growing collard greens." Sarah placed a towel around the shoulders of a volunteer. "You know how we turn the soil before planting?"

The women nodded.

"Who can tell me why we do that?"

A woman's hand shot up. "I do, Madam Walker! We loosen the soil so that all the good nutrients can get down to the roots."

"That's exactly it." Sarah parted the volunteer's hair with a skinny comb. "See this here? That's dead skin." She pointed to the white flakes on the volunteer's scalp. "Hair can't grow if dandruff is blocking all those nutrients from getting in."

Sarah worked through the hair, gently parting the strands and removing the dead skin as she went. Then she had her students divide into pairs and practice on each other. She taught them her secret methods for shampooing and combing hair. She taught them how to style the hair in a way that would protect it. She taught them techniques to help hair grow. By the time Sarah finished, every woman in the room was a certified Walker Agent.

"Welcome to the Walker family," Sarah announced, as she handed out paper certificates stamped with her official seal of approval.

Sarah loved listening to the murmur of voices and click-clack of feet leaving her workshop. She imagined each woman marching herself home and starting her own salon. Each agent could make up to fifteen dollars a day instead of a dollar as a washerwoman. Armed with their new knowledge, anything was possible.

"Madam C. J. Walker's Wonderful Hair Grower is a Miracle!" read the headline of a local newspaper. "Ladies are showing each other how to depend on themselves!"

~

Unfortunately for Annie Turnbo, Sarah was much better at selling herself and her products. Even though their products were similar, black women were drawn to Madam C. J. Walker and the stories she told.

Sarah wasn't shy. She told everyone who she was and where she came from. "I was a washerwoman, and look at me now!" she always said.

Absolutely everybody was talking about Madam C. J. Walker. Her newspaper ads, presentations, workshops, and word-of-mouth advertising worked wonders for her business. But they worked a little *too* well. Charles and Lelia couldn't get the orders out fast enough!

"Good morning, Mama," Lelia yawned, coming down late to breakfast one morning.

"Aw, baby. You look like you were up half the night!" Sarah clucked her tongue in sympathy as she passed her daughter a plate of biscuits and bacon.

"I *was* up half the night," Lelia grumbled.

"We're two hundred orders behind," Charles called from his desk in the next room, flipping through a tall stack of papers. "We've got plenty of business, but we might start losing it soon if we can't deliver. See this here? The West Coast orders are taking too long to ship from the East Coast. People are starting to complain."

"Don't worry." Sarah stood behind her husband and squeezed his shoulder. She pointed to a *very* big number. "Look! We've got the money to keep our distribution center in the east *and* open our very own factory, beauty college, and salon. We just need a new location."

In 1910, Sarah opened the Madam C. J. Walker Manufacturing Company in Indianapolis, Indiana, smack-dab in the Midwest. A few tears of joy escaped her eyes as she held her husband's and Lelia's hands. The jingling keys opening the doors of her own building was one of the most satisfying sounds she had ever heard.

CHAPTER NINE

Sarah woke at dawn each day. She had a huge business to run and many employees to manage. Dozens of women sold her hair products door to door. Dozens more mixed the products, packaged them, and mailed them out to Madam C. J. Walker hair salons all over the country.

First, Sarah went to the laboratory to supervise the production of her hair mixture.

"More violet oil," she instructed the workers, dipping her finger into a batch to check if it was up to her standards.

Next, she went to the salon where she greeted the shampoo girls folding towels near the washing station and hair stylists rinsing hot combs. Customers started arriving at 6:00 a.m. sharp and did not stop coming until well after dark. Charles often stopped by to bring Sarah a small bowl of cornbread and beans, but she usually didn't have time to eat more than a spoonful.

When the day was over, Sarah's feet throbbed and her back ached. She eased herself into a salon chair as one of her employees swept up.

"This place sure was hopping today!" Lelia said, pulling up a chair beside her mother.

Sarah agreed and frowned, thinking about doing it all over again the next day. "We're going to need to hire a few new shampoo girls and stylists. I wonder if we could fit another chair over there . . . "

"Annie's opening a shop nearby," Lelia groaned, kicking off her shoes. "Are we gonna pick up and move again?"

"Absolutely not." Sarah waved the thought away. "I'll lower my prices. She can't compete with fifty cent scalp treatments and twenty-five cent shampoos! We can add some extra services for nails and skin."

"Take a break from all your genius work. I've come to escort y'all home for dinner." Charles stood in the doorway, grinning at them. He propped open the door to let some of the heat waft out onto the street.

The cool night air felt good on Sarah's cheeks, and she couldn't help but feel thankful.

Sarah was grateful to her husband for sharing the burden of the business with her, giving presentations in nearby towns. She was proud of Lelia, too, for keeping up business on the East Coast. And she was prouder still of all she had built.

~

When Sarah stepped into her shop a few weeks later, it looked and felt like a spa. The cracked vinyl floor was new and sparkling. Comfy leather seats and fluffy pillows replaced the worn wooden

chairs in the waiting room. A greeter offered lemonade and cookies to clients.

Sarah straightened the sign at the nail salon station offering hand massages. The soft scent of shampoo and lotion mixed with the sharper scent of nail polish and steaming hot combs.

Sarah had hired enough people that she did not need to work in the salon. She no longer feared Annie running her out of town either. She remembered doors being slammed in her face when she first started out, and hunching over the kitchen table in her cream-splattered apron. She breathed a huge sigh of relief that those days were over.

This is what success feels like, Sarah thought. *Madam C. J. Walker is here to stay.*

"Madam?" asked a small voice.

"Yes?" Sarah looked down at a girl who couldn't have been more than eight years old. "What's your name, sweetheart?"

"I, um, uh . . . B-b-belinda." The girl stammered so much the words came out all smooshed

together. "D-d-daddy can't work, and I'm h-hungry. M-m-mama said you have errands sometimes."

"Well," Sarah said slowly, "I suppose I do. Now take a deep breath and try again. Do you have a question for me?"

Belinda did what Sarah asked, looking her right in the eye. "You got any errands for me, Madam C. J. Walker?"

Sarah smiled and quickly scribbled a short list. She pressed a shiny silver dollar to Belinda's palm along with a scrap of paper. "Why don't you run on down to the store and get me these things? You can keep the change."

"Thank you Madam Walker," Belinda squeaked. She scampered out the door.

~

Sarah gave and gave to the people around her. At holidays, she handed out whole turkeys and baskets of squash and potatoes. When black people were turned away from white hotels, she opened her home to them. She hired as many shampoo and errand girls, factory workers, and Walker Agents as she could. But no matter what she did, it never seemed to be enough. Poor black people were suffering everywhere she looked.

Sarah set her sights higher. She wanted to put her money where it would impact the entire community all at once.

One morning, Sarah read a newspaper story about a local community organization. In it, the editor George Knox wrote: "The YMCA building is going to pieces. Other cities have raised money to build their own centers. We can do it, too. Give what you can to this charitable cause!"

The Young Men's Christian Association (YMCA) helped people in need. Men and boys could sleep there if they had no place to stay. They could take job training classes and play sports. There was even a small shop where they could work for nickels and dimes. But the building was old, and there weren't enough rooms to go around.

Why doesn't something like this exist for black girls? Sarah wondered.

After reading the story, she marched right into George's office. It reminded her of her husband's newspaper office back in St. Louis, but messier. Scattered papers coated the floor and broken pens were rolled into corners.

"I want to get involved in the YMCA project. What can I do?" Sarah asked over the sounds of clacking typewriters.

George stared at her in shock. He had no idea what to say to a woman who wanted to support a men-only organization. But he pointed her in the right direction.

The male committee members of the YMCA politely declined Sarah's request to join the organization or sit in on planning meetings.

"Women need not concern themselves with matters of finance," said one board member. "What did you say your business was again?"

"It's hair, sir," said the note-taker.

Sarah stood up and saw herself out because they all seemed to be laughing at her. This, she *would* not stand.

On the very last day of the fundraiser, Madam C. J. Walker pledged a thousand dollars to rebuild the YMCA. Again, George Knox's eyes widened in surprise. He pulled out his notebook for a story that was already forming in his mind.

"You're pretty successful for a lady," George said.

Sarah stiffened, her expression sour.

"What's your secret?" His pen hovered above a blank piece of paper, waiting for her answer.

She thought about it for a moment, then said, "I believe in black women."

As she walked away from him, her mind was already working. She wanted, no, she *needed* to gain the business community's respect. And she thought she knew just how to do it.

CHAPTER TEN

Madam C. J. Walker arrived in
Chicago riding in her very own
Ford Model T car. She wore her
best skirt and jacket, made of the finest, softest
wool, and a pair of shiny black shoes. After a
determined press of her lips, she straightened her
fabulous hat with its gigantic feather.

"Pull right up to the front, William," she
ordered her driver.

"Yes, ma'am," William replied. He hurried
around the side of the car and tipped his hat to her
as he opened her door. Sarah strode purposefully
up the front steps and into the building under a
sign that read: "National Negro Business League."

The founder of the league, Booker T.

Washington, was the most influential black businessman in America. Booker had access to powerful people from educators to the president of the United States. He encouraged black men to start their own businesses and gave workshops about how to run a company. If anyone could help Sarah find the respect she'd earned, she decided, it would be him.

Sarah had written to Booker many times, but each time he'd replied with a short rejection.

She'd sent him her company brochures, showed up at his conferences, and requested to be a featured speaker. But he always refused to let Sarah on stage.

Then Booker did something that made her furious. He invited several other hair culturists to speak at the Chicago conference but not Madam C. J. Walker, the most successful of them all.

"I *cannot* believe this man!" Sarah said, hands shaking when she found out.

Rather than ask Booker's permission to attend the conference, Sarah called her editor friend, George, who happened to be there that weekend. "All I need you to do is introduce me. I'll do the rest."

When the time came, George stood up and began to introduce her. But Booker cut him off before he finished. Sarah knew it was now or never.

"Surely you are not going to shut the door in my face," Madam C. J. Walker said loudly as she climbed onto the stage. "I know you don't feel that my business is worthy of your time. But it is. I went into a business that everybody said was impossible: the business of growing hair. Nobody believed it could be done, but I have proven that it can!"

The whole room broke into applause. But Booker stood unmoved.

Sarah's voice grew louder. "I came from the cotton fields of the South. I was promoted from there to the washtub. Then to the kitchen. And from there I promoted *myself* into the manufacturing business. I have built my own factory on my own ground. I am not ashamed of my roots, and they don't make me any less of a lady. I know how to grow hair as well as I know how to grow cotton."

She gazed out at a sea of faces. They looked back at her, nearly all of them male. Most of them looked amused, but some seemed angry that a woman had taken over the stage to talk about something as silly as hair.

Sarah took a deep breath and went on to reveal her sales numbers, the number of people she employed, the size of her factory, and her expected profits for the coming year. The faces below changed from irritated to incredulous.

There was more applause, louder this time, but Sarah didn't want people to clap for her. She wanted them to *listen*.

"Let me speak!" she said, aiming her next comment straight at Booker T. Washington. "My goal is not simply to dress up and drive around in nice cars. I plan to provide opportunities for black people!"

Rather than comment on Sarah's remarks, Booker called the next presenter onto the stage, as if Sarah had not said a word. Sarah was disappointed by Booker's reaction, but from the audience's applause she knew she had done what she came to do.

Madam C. J. Walker was well on her way to earning the respect she deserved.

CHAPTER ELEVEN

William turned the car up the long road that led to the cabin Sarah had once called home. A trail of dust rose like smoke behind the wheels. All around were fields of cotton, like a sea of tiny white clouds.

The sight took Sarah right back to when she was a little girl. She remembered how she'd run through the rows chasing after Louvenia. Papa hoisted the overstuffed bags of cotton onto his shoulders. Over on the porch, Mama hummed her favorite gospel as she tucked fabric over her hair. Her three brothers, Alexander, James, and Owen, dangled their legs off the side of a rickety wooden porch.

Tears welled in Sarah's eyes as the memories overtook her.

"Ma'am?" William asked, stopping the car.

Sarah dabbed at her eyes. "I'm all right." She gave William a reassuring smile. "Drive around back. My mother and father are buried behind the house, and I'd like to leave a few flowers for them."

She didn't linger. Being there felt like a step back in time, where hands deliberately held her back.

On the drive out of town, Sarah read what the local papers had written about her visit. A white-owned paper had gotten it *all* wrong. They'd called her "Winnie" instead of Sarah, and referred to her as a "negress" who was "quiet and unassuming." Worst of all, they said that she specialized in *straightening* hair instead of growing it.

Sarah tossed the paper onto the seat beside her. She was glad to leave her hometown behind. She didn't have time for small-minded people. Besides, she had work to do thinking up new products, recruiting and training Walker Agents, giving lectures on hair styling at black colleges, and sharing her story with women everywhere.

But all the travel had started to wear on her. Sarah didn't want to admit it, but she felt tired. She was dizzy, too, with frequent headaches.

"I don't know what's come over me lately," she said to William as they stopped by a set of train tracks. "Maybe I'm not getting enough . . ."

Sarah's words trailed off seeing a man on the other side of the tracks, yelling and waving his arms. She couldn't hear what he was saying but there was terror in his eyes. A frantic train whistle made her jump.

Sarah spun around just in time to see a freight train hurtling right toward them! She screamed as William stepped on the gas. The car jerked forward so fast that his hat flew off his head. The train missed the car by inches.

Sarah and William barely escaped with their lives.

Even though she was out of danger, Sarah's

heart wouldn't slow down. In the days that followed, Sarah's dizziness and headaches got worse, so she visited the doctor.

"Madam Walker, I must insist that you cancel your lecture series," the doctor told her. "You need no less than six weeks rest."

Sarah assured her doctor she would follow his advice. She checked herself into a spa in Arkansas where the hot springs were believed to have magical powers. Twice a day Sarah

wrapped herself in soft, fluffy robes and walked to the healing springs. As she sat in the warm water, she could feel her muscles loosening. Stress seemed to seep out of her pores.

~

Though Sarah did relax for a few weeks, she decided she couldn't slow down. Not just yet.

Lelia bought a townhouse in Harlem, New York City. In 1913, Harlem was a hub of black culture

bustling with restaurants, clubs, and gorgeous houses.

Meanwhile, Sarah and Charles had been spending more and more time apart. After Sarah returned to Indianapolis, they decided to divorce. So when Lelia established the Lelia College of Beauty Culture and the Walker Hair Parlour in the heart of Harlem, she began pestering her mother to move there.

New York was the biggest city Sarah had ever seen, with sweeping gardens and giant fountains and buildings so tall they seemed to scrape the sky. Instead of streetcars, the avenues hummed with underground trains. Each time she visited her daughter, Sarah thought the move seemed like a better and better idea. It still took three years for Lelia to convince her. But, after taking a look at the rising sales numbers from the East Coast, opening a second headquarters in New York City made sense.

In 1916, Sarah left Indianapolis behind and moved in with Lelia.

One morning, Sarah stood over the stove in Lelia's

kitchen and dropped four pieces of bacon in the cast iron skillet. The bacon crackled and popped as the heat drew out the meat's grease.

Sarah filled a plate with her daughter's favorites: homemade rolls, honey, scrambled eggs, grits, bacon, a glass of orange juice, and two peppermint sticks.

For so long, Sarah had been busy traveling, giving lectures, and growing her business. She'd even begun partnering with groups like the NAACP to work on anti-lynching efforts. Today, she decided, would be devoted to Lelia.

I wish Moses was here to see all this, Sarah thought, remembering life with Lelia's father. Smiling, she headed to Lelia's room.

"Good morning, baby," Sarah said, as she set the breakfast tray on the bedside table.

"Good morning, Mama. Or should I say *Madam* Mama?"

"Hush, child."

"I'm glad you're home, Mama," Lelia said, laughing as she picked up a peppermint stick.

"What are these for?"

"To remind you how sweet life is when we're together," Sarah replied. She took the other stick and sucked on the end. "Now, eat your food. I have a surprise for you."

That afternoon the two got dressed in their finest and went to Tiffany's, the famous jewelry store. There, a saleswoman showed Lelia and Sarah diamond necklaces, rings, bracelets, and earrings in a private room.

"Pick something that suits you, baby," Sarah said.

Lelia ran her fingers across the glittering jewelry, choosing an ivory cat pendant with blue diamond eyes. Sarah bought herself a pair of diamond hair clips.

After they left the store, Lelia treated her mother to dinner, then the two of them strolled down the street, arm in arm. Their new jewels sparkled in the street lamps' glow.

Sarah snuck a peek at her daughter. Her businesses and work were important. But right there in that moment, all that really mattered was Lelia.

CHAPTER TWELVE

In the heat of the summer sun, Sarah stood in a sea of protestors she'd helped prepare for battle. They had all gathered for the same reason: to demand an end to lynching in America.

"Remember why we're here," voices shouted in the crowd before they all fell silent.

Across the river from where Sarah had lived in St. Louis, white mobs had lynched at least thirty-nine black people, injured hundreds more, and burned down homes and businesses. Sarah's anger had not dimmed through those years. She'd grown even more furious, and wouldn't let anything stand in her way. It still hurt her heart to remember how her first husband, Moses, had disappeared in the middle of the night.

Lord only knows what they did to him, Sarah thought. *That shouldn't happen to anyone ever again.*

As they marched, more and more people joined until there were ten thousand marching and twenty thousand more lining the streets. They protested in silence to pay respect to the victims, every mouth closed shut. The only sound was the shuffle of feet as they swept toward the center of the city, like a gigantic ocean wave, ready to change history.

After the protest, the United States government did not respond. So Sarah and the organizers of the silent march hustled themselves on a train headed for the White House.

President Woodrow Wilson had agreed to meet with them, and they intended to make their demands known at that meeting. They wanted the president to make lynching a crime and prevent it from happening ever again.

"We love America," Sarah said, as she and the

other black leaders walked up the marble steps of the White House. "It's time America loves us back."

Sarah felt her hopes soar as they were ushered into the magnificent building. Her heart beat faster with every passing minute, thinking about what she was going to say to the most powerful man in the country.

She nearly jumped out of her seat when the door opened.

"I'm sorry, but the meeting has been cancelled," a messenger told them. "The president is working on a bill for the Department of Agriculture and doesn't have the time to see you."

Sarah's ears started ringing, as if another headache was coming on. The president of the United States had decided that seeds and manure were more pressing than the lives of black people!

Her insides twisted with rage.

~

Fury still coiled in Sarah's belly as she thought about what she was going to say in her big speech at the 1917 Madam C. J. Walker Beauty Culturists Union in Philadelphia.

Two hundred women flooded the conference center wearing their finest clothes. With long, healthy hair, each was proof of what Sarah's products could do. Dozens of women stepped onto the stage to tell their stories, of how they had gone from maids to community leaders, from working their fingers to the bone to accomplished saleswomen.

"I can feed my family *and* send my boy off to college this year," one woman proclaimed.

"I was so grateful to put down my scrub brush and pick up a hair brush," another said. "My salon is the most successful in town!"

When Madam C. J. Walker finally took the stage, the room exploded with excitement. First, Sarah gave away prizes to those who had trained the most new agents, who had the highest sales, and who had recycled the most tins. The prizes motivated her agents to sell more products and work harder at their salons, bringing the company even more profits.

Then it was time for her speech.

Sarah knew just what she wanted to say. She told the story about her failed meetings with the YMCA board, with Booker T. Washington, and the president. She told the story of all the doors that had been slammed in her face. Because she was black. Because she was a woman. Because she was poor. But when she'd put her mind to it, she had built the biggest hair product empire the country had ever seen. And she *had* to use all of that money and influence for something positive.

"This is the greatest country under the sun," she stated passionately. "But we must not let our love of country stop us from protesting against injustice. We must resist until massacres like what we saw in St. Louis are rendered forever impossible!"

The women at the convention were so moved by Sarah's speech that they wrote a letter to the president. The letter demanded that the government ban lynching in America forever.

The president did not change the law. But Madam C. J. Walker had done something great. She'd shown a group of women that they, too, were powerful.

CHAPTER THIRTEEN

S arah loved living with Lelia in Harlem, but it was time to settle into a place of her own. She chose a neighborhood just north of New York City, where the rich Tiffany and Rockefeller families would be her neighbors. Sarah didn't know if they would be happy to have a former washerwoman living among them, but she didn't care. She was the most successful black businesswoman in the country and wanted everyone to know it.

"My house must be grand! Thirty, no, thirty-*four* rooms. It must feel like the luxurious palace of a queen," she told the famous black architect, Vertner Tandy, as they walked up the grassy patch of land she'd bought for her new home. "White

stucco walls! Greek columns! Balconies . . . one on either side! A sweeping front lawn here, and a gated driveway . . . "

Sarah stepped through the dewy grass with purpose, and Vertner had to hurry to keep up with her. The architect tripped on an exposed root, scrambling to stay on his feet, but Sarah did not slow down. "Come along, Mr. Tandy. I want the swimming pool here, a two-story patio here, and the fountain there . . . "

The architect pushed up his glasses as he jotted down more notes, adding to his nearly-full pad of paper. He bobbed his head at Sarah's every whim. Whatever Madam C. J. Walker wanted, she would get.

"Off this side, I want a grand ballroom," Sarah said. "Spare no expense, Mr. Tandy. And make sure that the dining room and sitting rooms can hold at least thirty people each. I expect I'll be entertaining often. Especially around the holidays."

Sarah clapped her hands together then pressed them to her mouth. She felt like dancing as she gazed over her very own land. She wondered what her parents and Moses would think. "I wish you were here to see it," she murmured.

"What was that, Madam Walker?"

"Nothing, Mr. Tandy. Let's get to work."

~

Lelia usually found her mother in her garden when she came to visit. Sarah loved her new home with its sweeping terraces, high ceilings, and gorgeous artwork, but she especially loved her garden. She put on her overalls and got to work, bending down in the shadow of her towering mansion like she was ready to pick cotton. The only difference was that Sarah now wore her hair loose. She hadn't wrapped it up in years, except at night in a silk scarf.

Sarah hummed as she worked. Though her health was fading, she still managed to get outside every day. She loved working the soil, pulling weeds and watching her seeds spring to life, just like magic.

"I brought you some lemonade, Mama," Lelia called. "You should let the groundskeepers do that."

"Hush, child," Sarah laughed. "It calms me."

The hem of Lelia's dress brushed the dirt as she helped her mother up. "I came to say goodbye, Mama, but I have time for lunch before I catch my train."

Madam C. J. Walker had hung up her feathered hat and was Sarah Breedlove again. Now it was Lelia's turn to travel all over the world. Her daughter was headed to Cuba, the Caribbean Islands, and then to Panama. Sarah wished she could travel with Leila, but Sarah's doctors insisted that she rest as much as possible.

Sarah set her gardening gloves aside and walked arm in arm with Lelia to the shade. "Travel well, daughter. I'll be right here when you get back."

Sitting beside Lelia, Sarah sipped a sweating

glass of lemonade and looked across her estate grounds. She thought about how far she had come from the fields filled with fluffy, white cotton. Now she was surrounded by fountains, flowering trees, and lovely blossoms.

She took a deep breath and let it out slowly. The air smelled of home.

AFTERWORD

Madam C. J. Walker (Sarah Breedlove Walker) died at age fifty-two in 1919, from hypertension and kidney failure. When she died, she was worth about $600,000 (equal to about $6 million today). She is now known as America's first female self-made millionaire. Her company closed down operations in 1981, but her famous brand was relaunched by Sundial in 2016.

At thirty-four years old, Lelia became president of the Madam C. J. Walker Manufacturing Company. Lelia traveled the world. When she returned to the United States, she decided to transform her image and renamed herself "A'Lelia." A'Lelia continued to live a glamorous life in Harlem until her death in 1931.

Before his death in 1915, Booker T. Washington eventually sought out Madam C. J. Walker as a donor for his Tuskegee Institute in Alabama.

At first, Sarah politely declined. Then she mailed him a five-dollar bill. Later, she provided many scholarships to Booker's students, and in turn he offered beauty courses at his university.

Annie Turnbo outlived Madam C. J. Walker by several decades, but her business never did as well. Today, Annie has been recognized for her role in inspiring the conversation around natural hair care for black women. Where before there were so few products, now dozens of brands line shelves across the country.

Before she died, Sarah had a special request of her land and property: "[My home] will be left to some cause that will be beneficial to the race—a sort of monument." The New Voices Foundation uses her mansion, Villa Lewaro, as a place where female entrepreneurs of color can learn to build, grow and expand their businesses.

Even in death, Sarah continues to support and lift up black people.

ACTIVITIES

YOUR EXCITING NEW PRODUCT

Madam C. J. Walker was an entrepreneur: a person who identifies a need and creates a business in an area that doesn't exist yet. You can be one, too!

Think about the items you use everyday (and they don't have to be beauty products!). List them here.

_____

_____

_____

_____

_____

Choose one example from your list, and explain why it stands out. Is the packaging appealing? Do you feel special after using it?

_____

_____

_____

_____

_____

_____

Now make a list of unique items _you_ need that
might not exist yet or could be improved.
(There might be more people out there who need
them, too!)

_____

_____

_____

_____

Choose one from this list and give it a name.
What does it look like? What does it do?

_____

_____

_____

_____

_____

TELL EVERYONE ABOUT IT

Madam C. J. Walker created ads and placed them in newspapers to help people discover her new product. This is a form of marketing, how businesses promote their products or services to customers.

Now, it's your turn! Think about your product. Why would someone want to buy it? Then draw your ad in the box below:

YOUR ELEVATOR PITCH

When Annie Turbo knocked on Sarah's door, she had only a few seconds to convince Sarah to pay attention. Nowadays, we call this an "elevator pitch," which is a brief, persuasive speech to get someone excited about your product or your business. A good elevator pitch should last no longer than a short elevator ride! Fill in the blanks below.

I am _____, and I'm known for _____.

I make _____ that does _____. I hope to use it to help people _____.

My product is unique because _____ _____.

Now, practice your pitch on a family member or friend!

iFundWomen

We are proud to announce a collaboration with iFundWomen on these activities.

iFundWomen is the only crowdfunding platform designed specifically for female entrepreneurs, providing access to capital, coaching, creative, and connections critical to launching and growing better businesses. Crowdfunding is when an entrepreneur raises small amounts of money from lots of people that they know to reach a specific goal amount.

Head to **iFundWomen.com** and check out female entrepreneurs who are raising money for their businesses right now.

ACKNOWLEDGMENTS

We couldn't have created this series without the incredible women who inspire us. Madam C. J. Walker changed the face of business with tenacity and determination. We love her entrepreneurial spirit!

Thank you, Denene Millner. You tackled the hard subjects in Madam C. J. Walker's life with care and attention. You are a legend in your own right. Thank you, Salini Perera. You created such beautiful illustrations. Monique Aimee, the cover lettering is gorgeous! And thank you to our brilliant copyeditors and proofreaders Susan Nicholson and Taylor Morris.

To iFundWomen, your support and partnership have been amazing. We are thrilled to have you on board for this exciting project.

And to the Rebel Girls of the world, we are nothing without YOU. Your support is what keeps us aiming higher and fighting harder. Keep resisting, keep pushing, keep creating!

ABOUT REBEL GIRLS

Rebel Girls is a cultural media engine on a mission to balance power and build a more inclusive world. It is best known for the wildly successful book *Good Night Stories for Rebel Girls*, a collection of one hundred tales of extraordinary women throughout history.

Good Night Stories for Rebel Girls, published in 2016, was an overnight sensation, becoming the most successful book in crowdfunding history. The title has since been released in over eighty-five territories around the world. Following the book's triumph, Rebel Girls released *Good Night Stories for Rebel Girls Volume 2* and *I Am a Rebel Girl: A Journal to Start Revolutions*. Good Night Stories for Rebel Girls is also a podcast, highlighting the lives of prominent women with beautiful sound design.